www.bigidea.com

Zonderkidz®

The children's group of Zondervan
www.zonderkidz.com

Tale of Two Sumos
ISBN: 0-310-70933-4
Copyright © 2004 by Big Idea, Inc
Illustrations copyright © 2004 by Big Idea, Inc.

Requests for information should be addressed to:
Zonderkidz, Grand Rapids, Michigan 49530

Editor: Cindy Kenney
Art Direction & Design: Karen Poth

Printed in China
04 05 06 07/HK/4 3 2 1

TALE OF TWO SUMOS

Written by
Karen Poth

Illustrated by
Tom Bancroft

Based on the VeggieTales® video "Sumo of the Opera"

BIG IDEA
BOOKS®

Zonder**kidz**

"What a day, wrestling fans! I'm Jim Gourdly from the Veggie Sports Network, coming to you ringside where we have just witnessed the unbelievable.

"Sumo champion wrestler, Apollo Gourd, has just knocked his challenger out of the ring with a single, crushing *belly bump*. This contest was Apollo's last stop before the final championship round with heavyweight, Po Tato. But all that has changed.

"In a crazy turn of events, an unknown wrestler defeated Po Tato in an unscheduled sparring match. His name? The Italian Scallion. The question on everyone's lips tonight:

"Who is this Italian Scallion?"

The Italian Scallion is actually... a cucumber—a cucumber who wears a hat that looks like the top of a green onion. The Italian Scallion is Po Tato's long time sparring partner, and he isn't even very good at that. Po Tato just likes having him around because... well... The Italian Scallion is a funny guy!

So how did this happen? Completely by accident. And this is where our story begins.

"I made him laugh really hard and he slipped on a banana peel and fell right out of the ring," the Italian Scallion explained to Po Tato's trainer, Mikey.

"Ohhhh, my aching back." Po Tato moaned from the ground.

"Look at you!" Mikey scolded the cucumber. "You're always joking around. And now I've lost my best wrestler for the championship!"

"You say you want to be a champion Sumo, but the minute the training gets hard, and it looks like you have to work at it, you give up. You never finish anything... unless it's a punchline. What are we going to do now?"

Mikey was right. The Italian Scallion was never able to finish anything. Just last month he had promised his friend, Hadrian, that he would fix his bicycle. But that never happened. Hadrian was still having to walk his paper route, longing for the day he'd have wheels again.

"You're just a silly cucumber," Mikey said. "You don't understand that you can't replace hard work with silliness."

Due to his silliness, the Italian Scallion would now have to face Apollo Gourd in the Sumo Wrestling Championship just two weeks away. This was no easy feat. No one had ever stayed in the ring with Apollo Gourd for more than eight seconds. The enormous gourd's belly bump had finished off every opponent who had ever hopped in the ring with him.

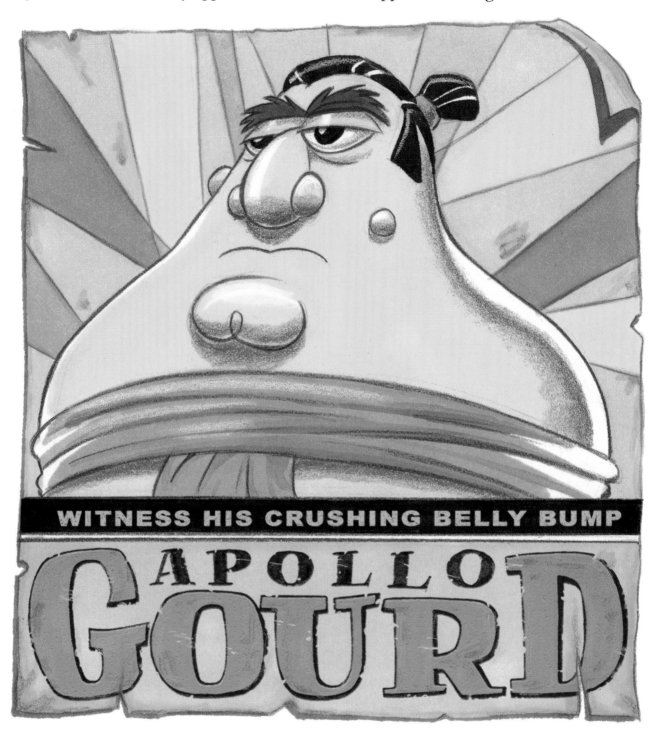

WITNESS HIS CRUSHING BELLY BUMP

APOLLO GOURD

"You have just two weeks to train for this match, Scallion," Mikey explained. "You'll never be able to stick with it and see it through to the end."

The Scallion felt a chill run up his spine. Mikey was right. He would never be able to last in the ring with the champ. **Unless...**

Scallion's face lit up. He had an idea. "Mikey, if *you* help me train," Scallion pledged, "I promise I won't give up."

"Really?" Mikey asked. "No matter how hard it gets?"

"No matter how hard it gets," the cucumber agreed.

The Scallion was sure that if he trained as hard as he could, he would be able to knock Apollo Gourd out of the ring. And the prize for winning the fight was a brand new Tiger Bike. He could give that to Hadrian for his paper route!

The Scallion smiled. He was determined to see this through. For Mikey. For Po Tato. For Hadrian. And for himself.

The next day the training began. Mikey and Scallion arrived at the gym bright and early to work on drills to get him in shape.

Each day, the training got harder...

and harder...

and harder...

Meanwhile... back at the gym, the champion did not take his new challenger very seriously. Apollo Gourd sat on his gym bag eating cheese curls.

"I do not need to train to fight this Italian Scallion!" he told his trainers. "I can beat him in my sleep."

But Scallion's training got **even harder...**

He **ate** like a champion.

He **exercised** like a champion.

He worked like a champion. But working was...well...it was hard! The Scallion became more and more tired and felt like he couldn't do it anymore. Suddenly, he stopped working.

"I quit," Scallion said. "It's just too hard."

"Look, Scallion," Mikey told him. "Sometimes there's a good reason to quit, but not just because it's hard. God asks us to do many things that are hard. But these things make us better and stronger."

Mikey followed Scallion as he headed for the door.

"Most things worth having take perseverance," Mikey added. "That means sticking it out to the end, even when it's hard to do. Perseverance, Scallion, **perseverance.**"

But the door closed. The Italian Scallion was gone.

On the street outside the gym, Scallion hung his head low. He had given up again... and it didn't feel good.

"Hi, Scallion!" Hadrian called out as he hopped up to his friend. "Look at the hat I made for show and tell!" Hadrian had a very strange hat on his head. "It's a scallion hat, just like yours. I'm wearing it because I'm so proud of you. You're a hero!"

"Th-th-that's great," Scallion said, a little embarrassed. "But you don't have to wear that hat for me. I don't feel like much of a hero."

Scallion couldn't tell Hadrian that he quit. He didn't want to disappoint the little asparagus...
again. Then Scallion looked at his friend's hat and thought about the bicycle parts in his
garage. Suddenly he had a change of heart. He realized that he had to finish what he had
started. He couldn't keep letting his friends down. He couldn't keep letting himself down!

"Yo, Hadrian," Scallion said. "I've gotta get back to my training. I'm going to win that
bicycle for you. I'm keeping my eye on that Tiger."

So Scallion went back to his training. Only this time, **it was different.**

The day of the championship fight finally arrived. Hundreds of Sumo fans came to the arena, each one expecting to see the Italian Scallion get bounced out of the ring with a single belly bump from Apollo Gourd.

"This is Jim Gourdly for VSPN reminding you that the first Sumo to toss his opponent out of the ring, wins the championship belt and the beautiful Tiger Bike.

"But don't get too comfortable folks, this match probably won't last more than eight seconds."

The bell rang!

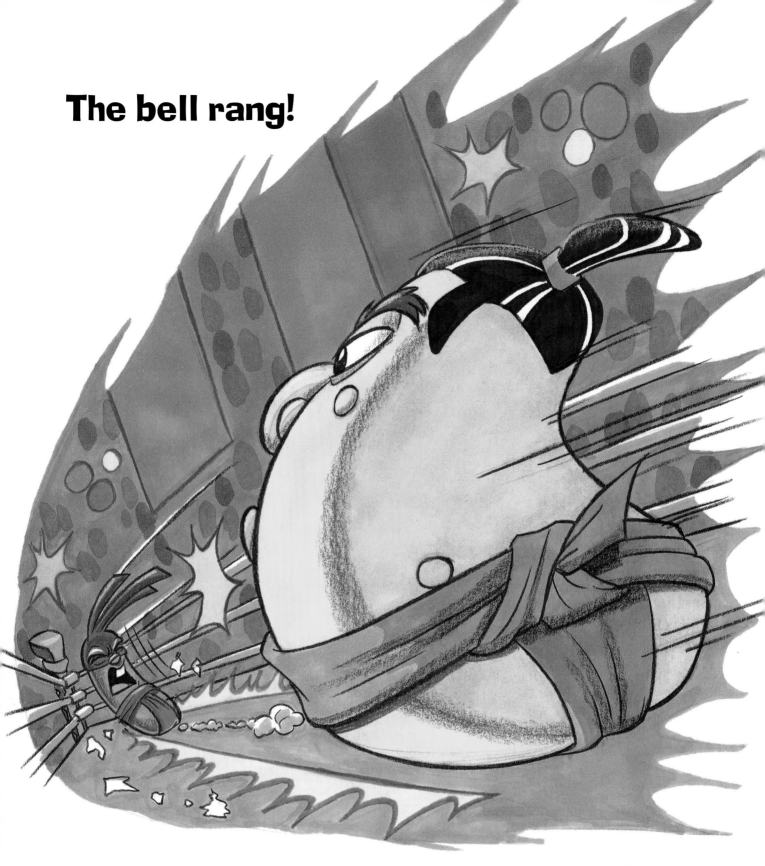

The Italian Scallion and Apollo Gourd charged into the center of the ring. **CRASH!**

They both collided. Then Apollo pushed the Scallion toward the ropes, leaving smoking skid marks on the floor.

"Scallion is in trouble already," Jim Gourdly whispered into the microphone. "Apollo is pushing him out of the ring."

Just then, Apollo bounced into the ropes and flew into the air. He gave Scallion one of his famous belly bumps, but the Scallion didn't move.

"Ladies and gentlemen, it didn't work!" Jim Gourdly announced. "This is unbelievable! The challenger is still standing. Eight seconds have passed, and the Italian Scallion is still in the ring!"

But the Scallion sure was tired. As he looked around at the crowd, his eyes came to rest on Hadrian. He was still wearing his scallion hat because he was proud of what Scallion was trying to do.

Then Scallion looked at the Tiger Bike that hung over the center of the ring and thought: *I have to keep my eye on the Tiger!*

With that, Scallion took a run at the champion and belly bumped *him*! But the champion didn't budge.

"Mop the floor, kid!" Mikey called from the corner of the ring. "Mop the floor!"

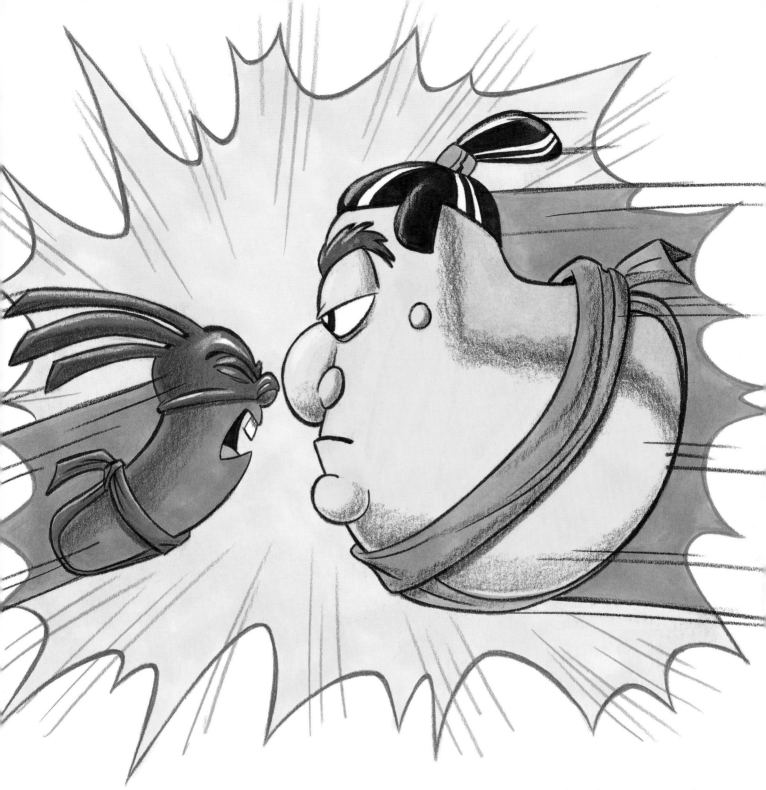

Remembering his intensive mop training, Scallion ran circles around Apollo. The giant gourd got very, very dizzy, until... **THUD!** He fell to the floor.

"This is amazing, folks!" Jim Gourdly reported. "The Italian Scallion was given absolutely no chance in this match, and now he's pushing Apollo Gourd toward the edge of the ring! He's going for the win!"

But as Apollo was moved closer to the edge, he suddenly sprang back up. The two wrestlers took one final lunge at one another. The collision was so incredible that they both flew out of the ring at the same time!

A hush fell over the crowd. Jim Gourdly could not believe his eyes.

"This is unbelievable! Both opponents fell out of the ring at the same time, which means this match is a tie! Apollo Gourd is still the champ. But what a performance by the Italian Scallion! No challenger has ever stayed in the ring this long. He's a winner in my book."

And that's exactly how the Italian Scallion felt. Even though he hadn't won the championship, he felt like a winner because he had persevered! He had finally stuck with something and saw it through to the end.

"I did it!" the exhausted Scallion told the reporter. "I persevered! And I feel **great!**"

Later that day, Scallion went to see Hadrian. "Yo, Hadrian!" he called. "I have something for you."

"You do? Did you win the Tiger Bike after all?" Hadrian asked.

"Nope. I did something else for you, instead." Scallion had put Hadrian's old bicycle back together.

"You fixed my bicycle!" Hadrian yelled.

"Yep," the Scallion said with a smile. "It feels great to stick with a project and see it through to the end. And now I won't be tripping over the pieces every time I go to the garage to put out my recycling," he added.

Even though Apollo Gourd kept the championship belt and won the Tiger Bike, the Italian Scallion was a winner, too. He learned that God wants us to finish what we start even when it's hard to do.

The Italian Scallion learned to PERSEVERE.